Christmas Tree Memories
by Aliki

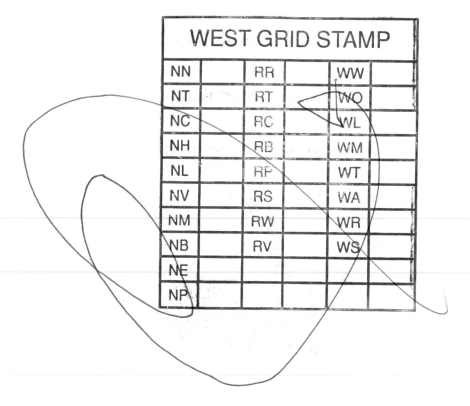

With thanks to Nancy Christoff
for the spark

First published in Great Britain 1992 by Methuen Children's Books an imprint of Reed Consumer Books Ltd
Michelin House, 81 Fulham Road, London SW3 6RB
and Auckland, Melbourne, Singapore and Toronto.
Originally published in 1991 by Harper Collins US
Copyright © 1991 by Aliki Brandenberg

ISBN 0 416 18719 6

Produced by Mandarin. Printed and bound in Hong Kong
A catalogue record for this title is available from the British Library

Merry Christmases
to
John Locke Marshall

TINNG. TINNG.
The children heard the bell.
It was the signal.
They peeked through the half-open door.
There stood the tree, glowing with candles,
its branches heavy with decorations.

Tomorrow – Christmas Day – they would tiptoe down to
the pine-scented room to see what presents Santa had brought.
But tonight – as always on Christmas Eve – this family sat
before the tree, sharing memories.

Some of the ornaments were older than the children.
But most of them the family had made,
some together with friends.
Each brought back a memory.

There is my heart of dough.

You were only two when you made it.
That was the year of the blizzard. Remember?

There was no water or electricity, and we boiled
snow for the soup and told stories by the fire.

Nefi was just a kitten then.

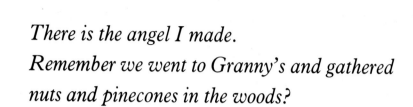

There is the angel I made.
Remember we went to Granny's and gathered
nuts and pinecones in the woods?

Then we went home and baked biscuits.
And I made the walnut cradle.

Aunt Eunice brought an ornament every year.
She brought the lion and the lamb when you
were just babies.

Then she got sick and died, but I remember her.

Remember we made "stained-glass" biscuits
in nursery school, and the mice escaped and ate
most of them up?

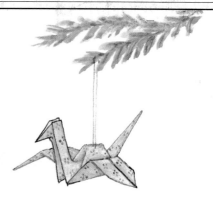

One year it was origami.
A lady at the museum showed us
how to fold paper into all kinds of shapes.

We made cotton-reel figures the time we had chicken-pox.

We made a tent over our beds, and you brought us
hot soup and sage tea.

We learned about corn that year.
Jolly showed us how to make wreaths from husks
when we all went to the country together.

Then we strung cranberries, and baby Nell sat on them.

And we all painted eggs.

Bobby gave us his but it broke
and you glued it together.

There's Bobby's starfish Santa.

*Remember the summer we went diving
and collecting shells?*

You made a mobile from them.

That year I banged my sledge into a tree
and was bandaged like a mummy.

And you learned to crochet decorations like Esther.

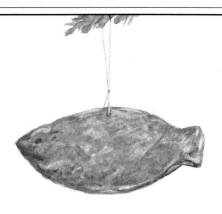

There's the fish we made of candle drips,
with Steve and May that New Year's Eve.
We woke you to see the fireworks,
but the next day you didn't remember.

The rocking horse is from Aunt Ann and Uncle Peter.

*Remember the summer at Yiayia and Papouli's
when Cousin Gregory lost his tooth in a pillow fight?*

*Papouli whittled the drum for me and the bell for you.
He made the best spaghetti sauce!*

The candles blinked and died out, one by one.
They sat in the dark, quiet with their thoughts.

Santa's almost here.
And tomorrow everyone is coming
for Christmas lunch.
We'd better get to bed.

They climbed the stairs.

Did you leave a snack for Santa?

Yes, and one for Nefi.

Good night, they said.

Merry Christmas! Good night.
Good memories!

Yes. Good, beautiful memories.
They fell asleep thinking of them still –
and of what new memories tomorrow might bring.